THE
ELEPHANT ROAD

NICOLA DAVIES

with illustrations by
ANNABEL WRIGHT

Chapter One

Wilen sat on the back of his uncle Denngu's shiny motorbike. They flew along a road between tall buildings, so fast the neon signs blurred with their speed. All the lights of the big city spread out in front of them like a feast. Faster and faster they went, so fast that the bike left the ground behind altogether and began to fly...

Thwack! Wilen's head hit the floor of the hut and he woke up. Something had tipped him and his little brother Relip out of their bed. They lay together in a heap.

"What happened?" Relip whispered, sleepily. "Why is the floor tilted?"

Relip was right. The slivers of moonlight coming through the palm-weave walls showed that the whole room was sloping. The two boys kept still and listened.

Something very, very big was pushing at the corner of the sleeping hut. It made a low rumbling that Wilen felt in his chest rather than heard through his ears, and its deep breaths huffed through the gaps in the walls. It shuffled its feet, with a sound like someone moving huge sacks of rice over a dusty floor, and pushed the hut further over. The bamboo framework creaked and groaned and the boys were rolled around like beans in a box.

They came to rest against the far wall and Relip cried out.

"Stop it!" he yelled at the creature. "*Stop it!* Go away! Just *go away*!"

Wilen thought that shouting might make it cross, and that it would be better to be quiet, but when he put a finger to his brother's lips to make him hush, Relip pushed his hand away and said, "No! Grandpa says they can understand what we say." And he shouted again, "Go away! *Go away!*"

For a moment their hut was held, as if the animal was contemplating overturning it completely, but as quickly and easily as it had been picked up, it was dropped with a judder. Outside, there was a little more rumbling and shuffling, one long, last sigh and then silence. The boys held their breath. Insects and frogs churred and plinked in the dark forest. The night had returned to normal.

"Told you they could understand us!" whispered Relip.

Wilen didn't reply.

Their father came in from the next room with a lantern.

"You all right in here, boys?" His hair was standing on end like the leaves on a pineapple, but his voice was calm and strong. As the husband of the village chief, the Nokma, Father was the village headman and he had to be a leader when things went wrong.

"Yes, father," said Relip.

"Good. You get back to sleep; there's nothing to worry about. I'm just going to look in on Grandpa and a few other people. We'll check on the damage in the morning," said their father.

Mother joined him in the doorway. "Nothing to be afraid of," she said in her reassuring Nokma voice. "They're just passing through, like they've done before." She stroked the little bundle flopped on her shoulder and added, "Your little sister didn't even wake up!"

Wilen and Relip exchanged a smile: their baby sister's ability to sleep was already a matter of family legend, so it was hardly a surprise that not even elephants could wake her.

Chapter Two

Wilen woke early. He slipped out of bed and pulled on his school clothes. Relip could sleep on; he was too little to go to school. Outside, the sunlight slanted through the trees and birds called. Wilen liked the cool stillness of morning, when the forest seemed to hold his village in its big green hand.

He looked at the ground beside the sleeping hut. There were marks on the hard red mud where the elephant's feet had been. Wilen had seen tracks like this before. Most years, about this time, elephants passed by as they travelled between one forest reserve in the east to another in the west.

"The reserves are elephant palaces," Grandpa had explained when Wilen was small. "We live on the elephant road between them."

Living on the road to an elephant palace had seemed to Wilen like something to be very proud of.

Wilen's village, Umiamara, Grandpa had told him, was near a special spot on the elephants' journey: the only place where the river banks were low enough to allow them to cross. A narrow, wooded valley led from the edge of Umiamara to the crossing place and, once in a while, as the elephants travelled past, they shoved a house and made it shake a bit. Father always grumbled that elephants should leave people in peace, but Grandpa said that anyone who lived by a road was bound to see some traffic.

But in the last few years, the elephants had started to appear more often. Almost every year now, they raided crops at harvest time or knocked over a storage hut to take drying maize. Last year, they had trampled a jhum field* and destroyed a whole crop of eggplants. In a village a few miles away, a man had been killed when he tried to chase elephants out of his crops. The people of Umiamara had begun to worry about their giant visitors.

Wilen inspected the corner of the hut that the elephant had pushed. One of the walls was buckled and the end of the hut had been moved by about half a metre. Wilen felt a shiver go down his back. It was scary what elephants could do so easily. But it was exciting too; he wished that he had been braver in the night and had peeped out through the weave

---

*jhum field an area which has been cleared of forest so that crops can be grown.

of the walls to look into the face of a wild elephant!

Wilen crossed the clay yard between his family's huts and poked his head around the kitchen door. His mother was cooking, with his little sister strapped to her back – fast asleep as always. His sister didn't have a proper name of her own yet, she was just called Nono, like all little girl babies were at first. Pots bubbled on the stove, with all sorts of delicious smells coming out of them.

But instead of talking about last night's elephants, his mother frowned. "Why are you in your school clothes, Wilen?"

Wilen's smile went out like a snuffed candle. Of course. It was the holidays. It had been the holidays since before Christmas and would go on being the holidays for another month. He had forgotten. Ever since he'd had a growth spurt last rainy season, he'd been like this – always forgetting the most obvious things. In a few months he'd shot up nine centimetres so his body didn't feel as if it belonged to him any more; he felt clumsy and awkward. And as for his voice, it had become completely unpredictable, sometimes a squeak, sometimes a growl. Wilen had almost given up talking altogether to avoid sounding foolish.

Grandfather said it was all part of growing up, that he too had had a voice that came and went and "a brain like a cloud" when he was Wilen's age. But Father wasn't so understanding; he just got cross.

"Why don't you just THINK?" he'd say when Wilen had forgotten to do his chores again. Or "Speak *UP!*" when Wilen didn't answer questions.

But his mother was more understanding, even if she didn't say much when Father got angry. She smiled kindly at him now, and said, "Just go and get changed. I've got a job for you."

Walking to the jhum field along the dirt road would take all morning, so Mother had told Wilen to take a shortcut through the forest. "But you'll have to pay attention, Wilen," she'd warned him. "So you don't lose the path."

She was right. The path was steep and narrow,
and rather overgrown. Wilen adjusted the strap on
his forehead, so that the basket wouldn't slip and
spill the food for his father's and uncle's breakfast,
and concentrated hard on where he put his feet.

There were huge trees in this old part of the
forest, with trunks two or three times the span of

Wilen's arms. The path curved around them and he had to clamber over their roots. It was mostly quiet in the forest at this cool, dry time of year, so the only sounds were those of Wilen's feet on the dry leaves and pebbles. Then suddenly, close by, gibbons began to call! They were the family that always stayed near to the village. People liked to hear them. It was a sign that things were going well. Wilen peered up into the canopy. At last, he caught sight of them. The dark-furred father, his two almost grown-up sons, and the mother, pale as mist, high in a banyan tree. They had a new baby in their family, too. Wilen had seen the little scrap clutched to the grey fur of its mother's belly a week before. Its brothers didn't seem to like it much. They sat around sulkily in the branches nearby and never held the baby the way he and Relip cuddled their new sister. Wilen gazed up, wondering how the gibbon brothers really felt about their new sibling. Were they as grumpy as they looked or did they secretly play with it when no human was around?

The gibbon calling was a little half-hearted. In a few minutes, they quietened down and began to move off through the treetops, arm over arm, spidery against the mosaic of leaves. Wilen followed for a while, but they moved too fast. They disappeared into the canopy and his attention came back down to earth. Where was the path? There was no sign of it at all. He couldn't even remember which way he had come. Should he go to the left or the right? How had he let his silly brain wander off like that *again*?

Wilen looked all around, calming his beating heart and trying to work out from the position of the sun in which direction he should go. *Rrrrruuup*. A deep, soft rumble travelled through his body from the ground. Wilen stared ahead and realized that the grey space between the leaves and branches, just a few metres in front of him, was not grey space at all, but *live* elephants. As he peered into the greenery, Wilen could make out the heads, ears and rounded bottoms of at least three animals – one very large and two smaller.

A mamma and two of her children. They were pulling leaves down from a tree that was covered with big yellow seed pods.

There was no way the elephants hadn't sensed Wilen's presence. They would have heard his noisy footfalls and smelt his human smell; elephants after all didn't have those huge ears and big noses for nothing. So either they were just about to rush at him and trample him to death, or they were simply waiting to see what he would do.

It was rather different being close to elephants without the wall of a hut between himself and them. Wilen felt very small and very fragile. He knew that to keep safe, he should move away as quickly and quietly as he could. But he was frozen to the spot with fear and fascination. He was *so* close that he could actually smell the elephants' warm, vegetably scent and hear the crack and crush of leaves and bark as they lazily took their food. Sunlight dappled through the canopy and for a moment lit up the face of one of the smaller elephants. The creature was perhaps younger than Wilen himself, but still larger than his mother's kitchen. For a fraction of a second, Wilen saw its eye – bright brown – shimmering with life, and felt that it had seen him too. A tingle went through his whole body. Then something startled the mamma and she gave a short trumpet of alarm. Wilen thought his heart would pop out of his mouth. He turned and ran as if all the demons of the underworld were after him.

Chapter Three

The work of clearing the jhum field had been going well. It had only been left to go wild for a few years, so the trees and bushes hadn't had much of a chance to grow. Some of those that had been cut before Christmas were now dry enough to burn, and little bonfires dotted the clearing. Pretty soon, the plot would be planted with crops again.

It wasn't the state of the field that Wilen noticed first, but Uncle Denngu's lovely, shiny motorbike parked by the side of the track.

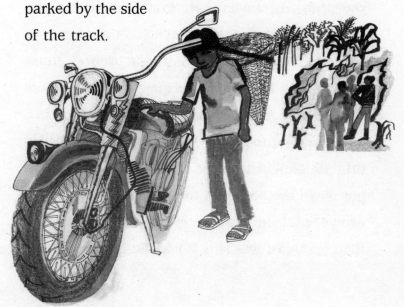

He walked past it and touched the chrome and blue metallic paintwork with one finger. What would it be like to own such a machine and to be able to go wherever you wanted? The thought of it made Wilen's heart race.

Denngu was his mother's youngest brother. He was as handsome as a movie star, and had a leather jacket and a mobile phone. Wilen hoped that, somehow, he would be like that when he was grown up. Denngu came from town to help out in the fields at busy times, but he never stayed long. He always had something more important to do somewhere else, but when anyone asked him what that was, he'd smile and say, "Business, business." Nobody knew exactly what Denngu did, or quite how he made so much money, but they liked him anyway.

Denngu stood with the other grown-ups, chatting. He smiled at Wilen and said hello when he put down the basket of food. With Denngu there, everyone was in a good mood, so no one asked why their breakfast was late. Wilen didn't want anyone to know that he had wandered off the path when he should have been concentrating. He hoped they wouldn't notice that the food was rather jumbled up in the bottom of the basket and scuttled off before anyone could find out. Denngu was busy with the grown-ups anyway.

A little way away from where everyone else brewed tea over the fire and chatted over breakfast, Wilen's grandpa was sitting on a tree stump. Denngu was Grandpa's youngest son, and they didn't get on. Grandpa was the only person who didn't think it was funny when Denngu said, "Business, business", in reply to questions about what he did for a living. But Grandpa always had time for Wilen, and never minded his clumsiness or his misbehaving voice. He beckoned to Wilen to join him.

"So, Nantong, come and sit by me." Grandpa was always inventing some kind of nickname for him. Skinny or Dreamy were the usual ones. Wilen didn't mind. He knew Grandpa was just being friendly.

Grandpa was very old indeed and as wrinkly as an elephant. He wasn't really strong enough to help with work in the fields any more, although he liked to watch over it and offer his opinions on how it should be done. But with the help of his stick, he could walk up and down the hill paths all day.

"What's the matter with you this morning?" Grandpa asked. "Did you fall over on the path?"

Wilen shook his head.

"What, then? You have sticks in your hair and muddy knees. Something must have happened!"

Grandpa always managed to ask a question that *made* Wilen say something, even if all he managed was a squeak, a growl or a whisper.

"Elephants," whispered Wilen.

"I know," said Grandpa. "There were elephants in the village last night, weren't there? But they'll have gone over the river by now!"

Wilen shook his head.

"No?" Grandpa raised his eyebrows. "You don't think so?"

"Elephants. Here," breathed Wilen.

"You saw elephants in the forest this morning?"

Wilen nodded and pointed back up the hill. In finding his way back to the path, he'd worked out just where he'd seen the elephants. And it was nowhere near the route they usually took down the valley to reach the river crossing.

"How many did you see?"

Wilen held up three fingers.

"Hmm," said Grandpa. "That's very interesting."

Wilen could tell that Grandpa didn't quite believe him. He felt a spear of anger leap up inside him like a sudden flame. Nobody took any notice of him any more! Sometimes, he felt like a ghost in his own life. Wilen left Grandpa sitting on his tree stump, picked up the empty basket and stomped back up the hill without bothering to say goodbye.

Halfway back along the path, Wilen put the basket down and headed off between the trees. He was determined to prove to Grandpa that he *had* seen those elephants. He wanted to prove it to himself too. The truth was that he doubted his wandering-cloud brain as much as everyone else seemed to.

He climbed around the roots of the big trees, concentrating hard on retracing his steps and on not getting lost, even for a second. If Grandpa were with him, it would be easy. Grandpa knew every bit of the forest around the village. He could name every plant and tree and could tell you a use for all of them. "This is good for flavouring fish," he'd say about some leaf or other, "and for curing fevers. And this is good for coughs."

Wilen couldn't remember which plant was which. He was much better at remembering the stories Grandpa told about the forest, and what lay beneath it.

"There are seven layers beneath the forest," Grandpa told Wilen. "Seven layers that you must travel through before you reach the underworld, where Sankani the giant snake lives."

Most of all, Wilen liked the stories about the

ancestors who had come to the forest from the high, high mountains.

"Our people were headhunters back then," Grandpa would say with a wicked smile. "They used to put the heads of slaughtered enemies in the branches of the biggest trees."

The story of their headhunting ancestors was one of Grandpa's favourites. Wilen wondered if any of those old heads were still up in the trees somewhere, and what it might feel like to find one.

In spite of his good intentions, Wilen found that his mind had wandered again. For a moment, he wasn't sure where he was and then he saw the tree with the yellow seed pods. *That* was where the elephants had been! Slowly, looking hard and listening at every step, Wilen walked around the tree. Leaves and bark had been pulled down all around the spot and there – in a pool of sunlight on the forest floor – were big, round dollops of poo. Elephant dung. He touched one with his fingers. It was still warm. The elephants *had* been real, but perhaps now they had headed down the valley to cross the river, like they usually did.

Chapter Four

For supper, Mother had cooked a meal of little fish from the river and pumpkin for the whole family, because Denngu had decided to stay the night before going back to town. Everybody crammed round Mother's dining table. Her sister, Aunty Em, was there, and her husband, who everyone always called Dax, their children, Wilen's almost grown-up boy cousins Toka and Tika and twin girls Salmi and Saljak, who were Relip's age. Mother's older brother Rengu, whose wife had been dead for years, was there too, and so were Mother, Father, Grandpa and Grandpa's very ancient sister-in-law who they all called Auntymama; plus Denngu and Relip and himself. Finally, there was little Nono, who was passed around the table to be cuddled and cooed over until she'd done what she was so very good at doing, which was fall asleep.

Denngu was sandwiched between Dax, who was always jolly and friendly, and Relip, who never ever stopped talking even though no one paid the slightest attention to what he said. Wilen loved it. It was almost like Christmas all over again, except that his two oldest brothers Kelip and Ruhap were back at college. Everybody talked and laughed all at once and Auntymama kept asking Grandpa what was being said because she was as deaf as a tree. Wilen forgot all about his cloud brain, his wandering voice and feeling like a ghost.

Afterwards, Mother, Aunty Em and Auntymama sat in the kitchen gossiping, whilst all the men took their chairs outside and sat talking around a wood fire. Relip fell asleep on Toka's lap and was carried off to bed. Wilen sat at Grandpa's feet and felt himself getting sleepy too as the conversation wandered to and fro with the wind blown smoke.

"We did well with the jhum plot today!" said Dax.

"Hmm," Grandpa snorted. "You should have left it fallow for longer. Fifteen years, we used to leave jhum fields to rest, when I came to Umiamara. Now it's only five."

"I know, I know," sighed Wilen's father. "But we have to feed everyone. We can't leave fields unused all that time."

"And crop yields fall every year," said Rengu. "Soon we'll have to cut down more of the forest to grow food."

There was a moment's pause and Denngu sat forward in his chair, his eyes shining in the firelight. "Why not clear some forest and make *real* money?" he said. "There's coal under all these hills. We could start mining and make a fortune. Enough money for proper Tarmac roads that you can drive cars on. Brick houses. Mains electricity. *Think* of it!"

There was a sharp edge to Denngu's voice and it seemed to cut away all the warmth and comfort of the fire. It was as if the air had suddenly grown colder. Wilen shivered and sat up, wide awake.

Grandpa drew himself up extra straight in his chair. "Brick houses and Tarmac roads in exchange for our forest!" he said. "That's your answer, is it? The forest gives us *everything*. It gives us rivers to drink from, rain for our crops, food, wood for our homes. Without the forest, who would we be?"

Everyone grew very still. Even the fire stopped crackling, as Grandpa and his youngest son squared up to each other like two cockerels in the yard, about to tear each other's feathers out.

"Ourselves, but richer," Denngu answered fiercely. "Not struggling any more."

"*Richer!* Ha!" Grandpa barked. "Is *that* what you think? Our hills stripped of their trees, our rivers dead and black with coal dust and chemicals. Our fields dried up and ravaged by all the wild elephants whose homes we'd taken." Grandpa stood up and so did Denngu.

"This is the modern world, Father," Denngu growled. "Forests don't pay and elephants belong in zoos."

They glared at each other over the flames for a moment then walked away in opposite directions into the darkness. Everyone drifted off to bed soon after that and talked in private. The sound of his parents having a long, intense conversation in whispers came through the wall but Wilen couldn't hear what they were saying. For a little while, Nono wailed and then, at last, everything went quiet.

Wilen lay awake, watching the bright moonlight slice through the walls like thin blades of silvery grass. Relip murmured in his dreams and pulled all of the blanket onto his side of the bed.

Now, Wilen was too cold to sleep. Silently, he pulled his shorts and sweatshirt on and slipped out into the night.

Chapter Five

Wilen walked down the track that led away from his mother's house. His moonshadow walked in front of him. It was skinny, with legs that were too long, but solid enough to show that he was real. The track snaked around the hilltop, skirting a valley where orange trees grew. Their last, few shiny fruits reflected the light, as if little moons were trapped in the branches.

He reached the lookout hut, from where the villagers kept watch for marauding elephants at harvest time, and climbed up the tall, bamboo ladder. The lookout had a roof, but not much wall, so you could see in every direction.

Wilen gazed out over the blue and silver moonlit land. The huts and houses of his neighbours stood, scattered through the trees, each in its own neat, swept yard. And all around the village, wooded hills stretched, layer upon layer, to the horizon, as if the houses floated on a sea of green, like a flotilla of boats on the peaks of waves.

When Wilen was very little, his world of wooded hills had seemed to go on for ever. But now there were holes in that world where the forest had been cut down to grow crops, and where fallow jhum plots were cut again before they had time to grow more than a few tiny saplings. The horizon was nearer than it looked, and just beyond it, roads and buildings, concrete and cars pressed ever closer. Sometimes, when he thought of Denngu's shiny motorbike, or went to the movies in town, Wilen wanted to be part of that big, busy world. And sometimes, like now, he wanted to shut it out and keep his family and his forest safe for ever.

Rrrrruuup. The unmistakable rumble of elephant conversation disturbed Wilen's thoughts. His eyes snapped away from the horizon. There, standing in the pond close to the bottom of the ladder, were seven elephants! He'd often heard Grandpa say how quietly elephants could move and here was the proof. They must have stepped out of the forest and up to the pond as he'd been climbing the ladder.

The elephants stood in the open, with every detail of their bodies visible under the full moon. Wilen was sure he recognized the three from the

forest: a big mamma and her two half-grown children. There were two other big ones – grown-up females, Wilen guessed – a medium-sized one and a tiny calf that huddled fearfully between its mother's legs. They all stood together in the water, filling their trunks, then squirting water down their throats. The baby wasn't very good at it and managed to squirt itself in the eye. Wilen had to put his hand over his mouth to keep his laughter inside when he saw that. The baby waved its trunk about and reminded him of Nono, and how she grabbed at things with her little fingers.

They moved out of the water, and for a minute Wilen thought that they were heading back towards the houses in the village and that he would have to raise the alarm. He grabbed the two old saucepans that were kept up in the lookout, ready to make loud, elephant-startling noises, but almost as his fingers closed around their handles, the elephants turned back down the valley towards the river and melted away into the shadows. At last it seemed they were safely on their road and heading for their next palace.

Wilen pulled his sweatshirt over his knees for warmth and stared out into the night. The moon-light picked out the shapes of the trees, and the stars shone and shone. He thought about Grandpa and Denngu facing each other over the fire. He *did* want to be like his uncle when he grew up, but Denngu was wrong about one thing: wild elephants did *not* belong in zoos.

Chapter Six

Wilen, wake up!" His father sounded cross. Blearily, Wilen opened his eyes.

"What were you doing up here on your own?" Of course, his father didn't wait for an answer. He was already halfway down the ladder. "Come on," he said. "Denngu's going to take your mother into Tura to sell her oranges and she wants your help."

Wilen sat on the motorbike in front of his uncle, almost on top of the handlebars, with Relip sandwiched in front of him.

"Don't hold me so tight!" Relip whined.

"Stop complaining, Relip," Mother told him. "Wilen has to hold you tight or you'd fall off."

Mother climbed on the bike behind her brother and just in front of several huge baskets of oranges that were strapped onto the back.

"You OK, Sis?" Denngu asked her.

"I think so!" Mother said. "Are you sure you've tied the baskets on tightly?"

"Well," Denngu laughed, "there's only one way to find out."

They shot off down the track. Relip and Wilen both screamed. Even Mother squealed like a girl. Nono, of course, was fast asleep on her back.

It was a lovely morning, sunny and cool, without a cloud in the sky and it was fun to be riding down the red dirt road instead of walking. They passed Aunty Em, Salmi and Saljak, with a basketful of tapioca roots that they were taking to sell beside the main road. Mother made Denngu stop, and they tried to work out a way of fitting Aunty Em on the bike too, but her basket was just too big and she waved them off, smiling.

Denngu was a skilful rider and he steered around the many ruts and bumps – the places where the rains would turn the road into a riverbed in a few weeks' time. In less than an hour, they were on the Tarmac road, speeding along with the wind in their hair.

* * *

It was already very busy in town. Tuk-tuks and cars wove in and out of the people on the streets, blowing their horns. The pavements were crowded with people selling things – fruit and vegetables, plastic bowls, pots, combs, rope, scissors and baby clothes. The shops were just opening – big hardware shops with huge metal pots strung up to the ceiling, little snack shops hung with strings of brightly coloured packets, like streamers.

Denngu dropped them by the taxi stand.

"Where are you going now, little brother?" Mother asked.

"Business to attend to. See you later!" Denngu grinned, but Mother didn't smile back.

Outside the hotel, they found a short stretch of pavement free and they set up their orange stall. Mother spread a clean piece of cloth on the concrete and Wilen showed Relip how to pile up the oranges in neat pyramids.

Mother bargained with every single customer, determined to get the very best price she could.

Before his voice had gone funny, Wilen had been an excellent salesman, always finding new ways to say how good his mother's oranges were, describing the tastes and smells of each different variety. Now, he didn't dare say a word and Mother was teaching Relip how to be her helper instead. She saw Wilen watching them and smiled sadly at him. "Here Wilen," she said, handing him a few coins. "Go and buy us some puris."*

Wilen wove his way to the puri stall. The street was full of people: ladies struggling with big bags of shopping; skinny water carriers with their funny, hip-wiggling walk (the ones that wiggled most were the best, and never spilled a drop); little strings of giggling children; men in lunghis* with enormous cardboard boxes balanced on their heads. Everyone was moving unusually slowly because a huge, black 4x4 was parked in the road, and they all had to go around it.

People flowed past the vehicle like water round

---

*puri a deep-fried flat-bread.
*lunghi a kind of sarong worn wrapped around the waist like a straight skirt.

a rock. Wilen was just a metre away from it, wonder-ing who could possibly own such a monster, when one of its rear doors opened and uncle Denngu stepped out!

But Denngu looked odd somehow. He was stoop-ing like a beggar as he spoke very fast to someone

in the dark interior of the car. His eyes darted about like something hunted. Wilen knew at once that his uncle didn't want to be seen, so he turned away quickly, but it was too late. He heard the car door slam, and a moment later, Denngu had struggled through the crowd to reach him. He put his hand on Wilen's shoulder.

"Hello, Nephew!" Denngu smiled the sort of smile that a tiger might give a deer before eating it. "You wouldn't tell anyone what you just saw, would you?" he said. "Even if you could," he added cruelly, "I like to keep my business quiet." He pushed some paper money into Wilen's hand. "Buy some extra puris, eh?"

Then Denngu was gone, and so was the big black car.

When he got back to the orange stall, Wilen gave his puri to Relip.

"But you love puri!" Mother exclaimed. "What's the matter, Wilen?"

Wilen just shook his head. Even with a proper

voice, he couldn't have described how things were churning round inside him: Denngu's horrible tiger-smile and the money, burning like poison in his pocket. It had taken his appetite right away.

By the late afternoon, Mother had sold all her oranges and her bag jingled with the money she'd made. Usually, on good market days like this, she'd buy them a little box of sweets to share with the girls – Aunty Em's twins – when they got home, but this time they walked past the sweet shop without stopping.

"Sorry, boys. I have to save my money today. We need to pay for our lanterns."

The village lanterns were solar powered. Batmi and Silbal who lived next door to Wilen's family rented them out and charged them from solar panels on their roof. No one liked to make Batmi and Silbal wait for their money as they were getting old and frail.

Wilen thought about the paper money in his

pocket. He could give it to his mother, but how would he explain where it had come from?

Denngu picked them up at the crossroads at the bottom of the hill. He looked like himself again. He smiled at Wilen as if nothing had happened and helped everyone to get onto the bike. Without the heavy baskets of oranges to slow them down, they zoomed along very, very fast. Relip loved it, but Mother didn't and asked Denngu to slow down. When his uncle just laughed and ignored her, Wilen wished that he had enough voice to shout at Denngu and tell him what to do.

Umiamara was buzzing with news when they got home. Uncle Dax's cousin had come up on his ancient moped specially to bring it: a herd of seven elephants had trampled several houses in his village, Gorapunji, in the night. Like Umiamara, Gorapunji stood on the elephants' road, only on the other side of the river, so Wilen knew at once which elephants were involved.

"I'm sorry for you," Father said to the cousin. "But it's a blessing no one was hurt."

"Yes," replied the cousin. "But a baby elephant strangled itself in the big new fence on the edge of the village. At least that's one less of the wicked beasts!"

"There's nothing wicked about elephants," Grandpa frowned. "Only humans can be wicked!"

Dax's cousin opened his mouth like a dead fish but Mother chipped in to stop any argument. "Tell us about the new fence," she said, smiling. "What does Gorapunji need a big fence for?"

Wilen could guess what had happened. A fence had blocked the elephants' road, stopping them from travelling peacefully between their palaces. No wonder the calf had got tangled up. Now it would never learn how to use its trunk properly.

"The fence was around the new coal depot in Gorapunji," Dax's cousin explained. "A business-man is paying us money to allow him to build a depot. It will bring jobs, also."

It was obvious that the cousin was very proud of Gorapunji's new venture, but now Mother's face too showed disapproval.

"Times are hard," said Dax's cousin grumpily, seeing their expressions. "Our jhum fields don't yield like they used to and we have to make money somehow."

"Huh!" Grandpa grunted. "I'm sure my youngest son would agree with you. Eh, Denngu?"

But Denngu was nowhere to be seen. They could hear his motorbike heading down the track towards the Tarmac road.

Chapter Seven

The cut weeds and stumps on the jhum plots dried out in the sun and were burnt to put some of their goodness back into the soil. Almost everyone helped with the planting of the new crops. Chilli and eggplant seeds were sowed first – planted the moment that the fires died down. Relip, the twins and Wilen got their hands covered in ash. Salmi drew tiger stripes on Relip's arms with her sooty fingers and then they all ran back up the track to the village with Relip the tiger roaring behind them.

That was the last day of the holidays. Wilen went back to school, walking down the track every morning to the schoolhouse in the next village. Most of the time, he walked alone because the older children, like Toka and Tika, set off to catch the bus to high school in town an hour earlier, and the younger children didn't go to school yet. Wilen rather liked his solitary walk. It was the part of his day when he didn't have to try to concentrate or

speak, two things that had been so hard since his
sudden growth spurt.

At school, he struggled all day to think in a
straight line and make his voice work to answer the
teacher's questions, or to talk to the other children.
Even playtime was a strain. But on his walk, he
could relax and let his brain flit about as it wanted.
He didn't have to worry about speaking to anyone.
He listened to the sounds of the forest, the birds

and insects, he watched the breeze moving through the leaves. When the rains came, he noticed the changes every day as the water and the warmth of summer brought everything back to life.

The jhum plots began to sprout with little shoots of gourds and pumpkins, maize and millet, spinach and tapioca. The scent of all kinds of orange blossom was everywhere, like a cloth of perfume woven from many different threads. Wilen shut his eyes and breathed it in. In the valley, the rice paddies turned brightest green. Hens and their fluffy chicks scratched in the yard and Mother's cow gave birth to a beautiful cow-calf. The grown-ups were busy in the fields, and after school and at weekends the children helped out. It was a lot of hard work, but there was always time to rest: when it rained so hard that all you could do was take shelter and watch the drips, or in the evening in the smoke of a fire. His parents read and reread Kelip and Ruhap's letters home by the lantern light. Nono got her first teeth.

The year went on as usual and yet, more and

more, Wilen got the feeling that underneath, things weren't quite right. There was a report in the local newspaper about elephants damaging crops near villages on the other side of the river. It was, the report said, happening more and more, and people were taking matters into their own hands. Three female elephants had been found dead from poison and another, a male, had been shot when he had knocked down a wall of the new technical college outside Tura.

Father sighed when he read the news. "Maybe Denngu's right. Maybe wild elephants *should* just be in zoos now," he said.

Grandpa told him that he was talking nonsense. "If someone built a wall in the middle of Umiamara," he said, "what would you do? You'd knock it down, wouldn't you?"

"It's not the same at all," said Father crossly.

"Yes, it is," said Grandpa. "It's exactly the same."

No one heard a word from Denngu. In fact, no one even mentioned him. Almost every night,

Mother and Father whispered on and on until Wilen gave up waiting for them to stop, and fell asleep. Grandpa began to be grumpy nearly all the time.

One evening, Dax's cousin came to visit and talked about how the fence that the elephants had destroyed had been mended and how the villagers were thinking of selling more land and turning another jhum plot into a coal depot. Grandpa shut the door of his house and didn't come out for dinner, even though Mother had cooked his favourite meal: pork with ginger.

Every time Wilen went into town, the lorries loaded with coal could be seen going up and down the main road, beeping their horns and overtaking on blind corners.

Then the weather took a turn for the worse, with rain so heavy that it washed away soil and seedlings, and the jhum fields had to be planted again. People began to get fevers and chills. Little Nono started to cough – a tiny, pathetic sound that made the whole family sad.

In school, they were learning about volcanoes and how the lava boiled secretly, building up and building up. Home began to feel just like that. Wilen waited for an eruption.

Chapter Eight

It came in the middle of the night.

Wilen woke to the sound of loud voices and the flash of torch beams. He and Relip leapt out of bed. Father was already dressed and standing in the yard with Dax and Rengu, Toka and Tika, and Nambat – their neighbours grown-up son. Rain ran down their faces and dripped off their chins in the torchlight.

"Elephants!" panted Nambat.

"Yes, in the rice paddy by the bend in the track," added Toka.

"How many?" asked Father.

Toka and Nambat looked at each other and shook their heads.

"Not sure. At least three," Nambat said.

"They could ruin the whole crop," said Dax.

"And it's our biggest paddy," Rengu added.

Grandpa stomped across the yard through the puddles. "Elephants? What are they doing here at this time of year?" he said.

"Stealing our rice crop," said Father crossly. "Right. Let's get down there. Not you, Achu. I don't want you outside in this rain."

Grandpa opened his mouth to protest and then shut it again. No one argued with Father when he was organizing things.

"Relip, get inside with your mother and Nono," Father barked. "Wilen, get dressed and come with us. You're big enough now to be useful."

Wilen's heart leapt; only grown men got to help chase animals out of the crops. He walked down the track with the others, glowing with pride, hardly noticing the rain that soaked him to the skin.

Just before they reached the paddy field, they put out their torches and moved silently between the betel trees* that flanked the field. Clouds shut out the moonlight and it was as dark as a cave, but the the rumbling of the elephants' talk and the squelch of their feet in the paddy could be heard over the pattering rain and the plinking frogs.

---

*betel tree a tall, skinny palm tree grown for its nuts.

"If we startle them now," breathed Dax, "they'll just run further into the paddy and do more damage."

"But if we chase them the other way, they could panic and run straight through the village," said Silbal.

"OK," said Father, "here's what we'll do. Dax! Rengu! You and I will go round to the other edge of the field, very quietly. The rest will stay here and climb into the trees with torches. We will make some noise and push the elephants this way towards the betel plantation, but not so that they panic. They'll have to cross the stream and the moment they do so, the youngsters will flash lights and bang pots. That should be enough to send them back down the valley to the river, where they're supposed to be!"

"It's that wretched coal depot," mumbled Dax. "That's what's sent them this way."

It was hard climbing a palm trunk that had no branches, with no light and a saucepan strung around your neck. But it had to be done. Staying at ground level with a herd of possibly very cross elephants coming towards you just wasn't a good idea. Wilen clung to his tree and strained his eyes into the darkness.

"The trunk's really wet," whispered Tika. "I'm slipping."

"Shut up and stop moaning, Tika," Toka told him. "Just keep a lookout."

"But I can't see anything!" Tika complained.

"There!" said Nambat. "I can see lights on the other side of the field."

Through the leaves and rain, torch lights flashed and the sound of saucepans being beaten rang out like gongs.

"I can't see the elephants," said Tika. "How will we know when—"

"Now!" yelled Toka. "NOW!"

The elephants had shot across the paddy field much faster than anyone had expected. They'd crossed the stream before the boys had spotted their huge shapes, darker than the darkness, crashing through the vegetation at the foot of their trees. At once, the boys flicked on their torches and began to make as much noise as they could. To be able to bang his saucepan-drum, Wilen had to let go of the tree with his right arm, and instantly he slipped. He dug the soles of his feet into the tree trunk, pressing so hard to stop himself sliding further that his leg muscles screamed.

Directly below, the elephants trumpeted in alarm and smashed into the betel trees. One collided with Wilen's tree, making him lose his grip.

He slipped, scraping the skin off his ankles and shins, and landed on the ground. His flailing torch came to rest shining straight ahead, lighting up the huge, body-crushing legs of an elephant. It was so close that Wilen could have reached out and touched it. He shrunk against the tree like a snail curling into its shell, expecting to be stamped to nothingness at any moment. The elephant's legs swung towards him in the torchlight and Wilen screamed. It was the loudest sound he had managed to make for more than a year. The elephant turned and ran. A moment later, the crashing of the herd's retreat faded down the river valley.

Father's plan had worked!

Nambat, Toka and Tika slapped Wilen on the back.

"It was your scream that did it!" said Toka.

"Yeah!" Tika laughed. "I didn't think you could make sounds that loud any more, Wilen," he teased.

Wilen tried to say, "I didn't think so either." But the "I" and the "didn't" came out as a low growl and the "either" as a squeak higher than a mouse's, so he gave up and just laughed instead.

Father, Dax and the others sloshed their way through the swollen stream and joined the boys.

"I don't know what you youngsters are smiling about," said Dax, gloomily. "It looks like we won't be eating much rice this winter."

Chapter Nine

As village leaders, Mother and Father called a meeting to discuss the loss of the majority of the rice crop. Everyone would come to the Nokma's house for a meal in the evening and talk. So Mother, Aunty Em and Auntymama spent all of the next day cooking. Mother's big pots came down off the shelves and a fire was lit in the yard to cook on, as not everything would fit on the kitchen stove. Wilen, Relip and the twins were kept busy peeling and chopping, washing pots and fetching water.

Father, Rengu and Dax, with Grandpa giving instructions, put up a shelter of bamboo and thatch, so that everyone could sit around and eat together without getting rained on. Denngu was mentioned for the first time in weeks and Nambat was asked to call him on his mobile phone. Nambat's phone always worked as he'd rigged up a way to charge it at the solar-lantern station in his parents' house.

Everyone was very glad to sit down around the

fire and eat Mother's delicious food, but when it came, the talk was pretty gloomy. Wilen listened to all the voices around him, like little strands of the same sad story...

"We won't be eating rice this time next year."

"If the rain washes another lot of seedlings away, I won't have a single eggplant to sell come harvest time."

"I'll have to leave the jhum fields and get a job in town, if things aren't better next year."

Wilen saw his mother and father exchanging worried looks. Mother whispered in her husband's ear and he nodded. As usual, she was telling him what he needed to say.

Slowly, Father looked around at all the faces, taking them in; everyone fell silent. "We've had a setback, that's true," he said. "But young people like Nambat here shouldn't have to think about leaving. It's true that our yields have been falling and it's true that we seem to be having more problems with elephants. But all we need are a few extra ways to make our land pay. Egg production, for instance, and honey—"

"That's all very well," Batmi interrupted, "but where do we get a chicken house big enough?"

"You need proper hives to keep bees," added Nambat.

"It all takes *money*," said Rengu, "and we don't have any, brother-in-law."

"Well," said a voice from the shadowy doorway, "it looks like that's where I come in."

Denngu stepped into the light. He seemed to have got taller and more handsome since they had seen him last. He was dressed from top to toe in shiny black biker's leathers. He looked even more like a movie star than ever. Wilen wondered if he'd bought an even bigger motorbike.

Everyone stared at Denngu, open-mouthed.

Grandpa was the first one to speak. "Well, you've made yourself scarce in all our troubles, Denngu," he growled.

Father looked Denngu up and down. "You

certainly seem to be doing very well ... for *yourself*."

"I've been working for you and for Umiamara all the time," Denngu replied. "I've been finding better solutions to your problems than a few chickens or some pesky bees." Denngu had always been cheeky, but this level of rudeness took everyone's breath away. Denngu simply took advantage of the silence. "I've been working to make a deal for you, even better than the deal I set up for Gorapunji's coal depot."

"If it's anything to do with coal," Grandpa snapped, "we don't want to know."

"Not coal," Denngu snapped back. "It's pineapples and tea. My business partner is willing to take as much as you can grow. He'll be here any minute and he'll tell you himself..."

Denngu had planned well. The words were scarcely out of his mouth when a huge black 4x4 lumbered its way into the village. Wilen recognized it at once. A man with pale skin and fat hands got out of the back of the vehicle. He introduced himself as Denngu's business partner, Dawki Patchap. He smiled a great deal and shook hands with all the grown-ups. His driver gave out small presents – packets of snacks and sweets, tea and soap.

Mr Patchap sat down like a king coming to be crowned and started talking. He talked about the money people in other villages had made and showed them photographs on a computer of the new houses and roads that doing business with him had brought. A bright future for them and their children was within their grasp. All they had to do was clear their forest and grow crops for him.

"Of course," Mr Patchap added, smiling, "I will provide chemicals to keep your crops free of pests. *All* pests." He hit a button on the computer and a picture of a dead elephant popped up on the screen.

After the loss of their rice crop, no one in Umia-mara liked elephants very much. But, all the same, an uneasy murmur passed around the fire at the sight of the poisoned corpse.

Denngu's eyes blazed.

"Why are you sentimental?" he said. "Elephants ruin your livelihood! The forest doesn't pay its way! So what could be simpler? Get rid of them both and be rich instead of poor!"

All this time, Grandpa had sat quietly, like a pot slowly coming to the boil. But now he struck the ground with his stick. Sparks flew off the stones. A terrible silence followed; Wilen felt it on his skin like the cold sweat of a fever.

Grandpa stepped up to Denngu so that they faced each other in the firelight.

"How could a son of mine be so stupid?" Grandpa roared. "The forest gives us *everything*: our homes, our medicines, the water we drink. The elephants and the gibbons are a part of the forest, just as we are. The forest gives us our soul. But maybe you don't have a soul any more, Denngu."

They were almost nose to nose. Their two faces, silhouetted against the firelight, were so alike and so furiously angry. Wilen thought they might hit each other.

Mother stepped in between them. She spoke to Denngu in a voice as cold and hard as a stone. "Step aside, brother. Let our father pass," she said.

For a moment, Denngu stared defiantly into his father's face, then he dropped his eyes and did as his sister had asked him. Grandpa walked out into the dark.

Denngu turned to speak to the whole village. "Make up your minds – and quickly," he said. "Mr Patchap and I will return in two weeks to hear your decision."

The big black car bumped off down the track. The moment it was gone, the villagers began to talk very loudly. Mother whispered in Father's ear again and urged him forward.

"Quiet, everyone!" Father shouted. "We all need

to think about this very carefully. Whatever happens, we must not let this create quarrels. We must come to a decision that we all agree on."

Far into the night, every house in Umiamara was filled with talk. Wilen could hear his parents' whispers, hissing like a barrel full of snakes. He tossed and turned, his thoughts swirling.

"Keep still!" said Relip.

"Can't," breathed Wilen.

"Then tell me, brother, who is right? Grandpa or Uncle Denngu?"

That was just what Wilen had been trying to work out. Grandpa was right. The forest did give them so much, but if they couldn't grow enough food to live on, then what could they do? Poisoning elephants was horrible, but if elephants ate crops, then people would starve.

"What's the answer, Wilen?" said Relip sleepily.

"I don't know," whispered Wilen, miserably. "I don't know."

Chapter Ten

Volcanoes, when they erupt, don't explode just once, but several times. Two days after the elephants had destroyed the rice crop, Umiamara experienced another, more terrible, eruption.

The warning was announced on the radio at lunchtime: a tropical cyclone that the weather forecasters had named "Isabella" was heading their way. It had raced over the Bay of Bengal and would reach their hills by the evening. Everyone was sent home from school. As Wilen walked up the track to Umiamara with his cousins and the other high school kids, the sky to the south was purple and yellow, like a big bruise.

Toka looked over his shoulder and let out a low whistle. "Wow! There she is – Isabella. She's certainly ugly!" he said. "I've never seen a sky like *that* before."

Everyone stopped to look. And then, without another word, they all turned and began to run up the track.

Mother was shoving chickens into a basket like so much dirty washing, to keep them from being blown away. Father was leading the cow and her calf into the dining room, because the rain shelter where the animals usually spent the night was not secure enough for this kind of weather. Relip tugged on the pig's rope, trying to persuade her to go inside too.

"Thank goodness you're home!" said Mother. "Quick, take this ladder to Aunty Batmi and Uncle Silbal and help them take the solar panels down."

Aunty Batmi was wringing her hands with worry. "Nambat's with his wife's family today and Silbal is in town," she said. "I hope they'll take shelter somewhere."

Wilen smiled at her and managed to say, "Yes, I'm sure they will," in a voice that he hoped was loud enough to be heard.

Batmi and Silbal ran the solar recharging station for the village lanterns, but Aunty was too old and wobbly to get up the ladder, so Wilen went up for her. The wind was already shrieking in the trees and it took all of Wilen's strength to unscrew the panels and lift them down from their pole.

"You are tougher than you look, Wilen," Aunty said. "Now, get home. The storm is almost here!"

The rain stung like sharp stones as it hit Wilen's skin and the wind tried its best to peel him off the ground and send him skeetering off like a leaf. He clung to trees and crawled on the ground. It took him half an hour to get home from Aunty Batmi's house – a journey that he usually skipped in five minutes.

When he got back, Father pulled him in through the door of their sleeping house. "I was just about to see if you had blown away, son!" He looked more pleased to see Wilen than he had in a year.

It was dark in the hut. Father lit the stub of a candle in a jar. They needed to save the lantern as they had no idea how long the storm would last. In the flickering light, Wilen could see Relip sitting in the corner with the basket of clucking hens, and

Mother on the bed feeding Nono.

"Where's Grandpa?" Wilen breathed.

"He's out in the forest..." said Mother. "He's collecting medicine plants for Nono's cough."

"Don't worry," said Father. "He knows many safe places to shelter from any storm."

But their reassuring words didn't hide the fear in their faces.

Night came, but no one slept. The house rocked and creaked as if a whole herd of elephants was worrying at it. Through the roaring rush of the wind and rain came sounds of tearing and falling as the storm ripped branches and leaves from the trees and threw them to the ground. Then, not long before dawn, came a terrible new noise. A kind of roaring and crashing, but so loud and on such an enormous scale that it was impossible to imagine what it might mean. All Wilen and his family could do was cling together and endure the vast, breaking wave of sound. The ground shook under their feet.

"Is it the end of the world?" Relip whispered.

Wilen thought it might be, so he just held his little brother tight, until it was all over.

Chapter Eleven

Sometime in the morning, when the sun was a watery patch in the grey sky over the hilltops, the family came out of their house. Wilen's first thought was that their hut had somehow been blown to a new place – to a hillside he had never seen before. Their kitchen hut and Grandpa's little house beyond it had simply gone, as if they had never existed at all. In their place was a vast, muddy gash. It looked as if the giant of all giants had dug a hole and then flung mud and rocks in a river of devastation down the hillside.

Now they understood the meaning of the noise they'd heard in the night. Relip buried his head in Mother's skirts and Wilen stood very, very close to his father.

"A mudslide," said Father, quietly. "Another few metres and we would have been swept away."

"We must check on everyone..." said Mother.

"Yes, yes," Father replied. "Assess the damage. Notify the authorities."

Wilen looked at his parents. Although they were pale with shock and exhaustion, they were already thinking of their roles as Nokmas, the leaders of the village. *They* would be taking care of all the village, which meant that *he* would have to take care of looking for Grandpa.

When his parents went off around the village with Relip and Nono, Wilen offered to stay behind in case Grandpa came back. But as soon as they were out of sight, he set off. He climbed down the side of the giant's pit, onto the surface of the mud-slide and picked his way over the jumble of rocks and soil and torn-up trees. Half the hill on which his home stood had simply collapsed, destroying a betel-nut plantation, his mother's orange trees and one of the biggest of the village jhum plots. The debris had blocked the stream and almost filled the valley, changing the landscape for humans and for elephants too. What would *they* make of it if they came back this way?

Wilen picked his way over the rocks and mud, searching for any sign of huts or animals. Surely the slide had cut through at least six of the seven layers that separated ordinary life from the underworld... Perhaps Sankani would stick two heads out of the debris! It cheered Wilen to think of that, to remember Grandpa's voice telling him stories, calling him nicknames.

A soft moo made him look up. There, under a tree that dangled upside-down by its roots, was their cow and her calf. Wilen ran towards them. They were covered in mud, and their eyes looked wild and frightened, but they seemed very glad to see him. Someone had tied the cow's halter to a branch with a twist of grass. Wilen's heart leapt. He felt sure that the someone must have been Grandpa. He dived under the tangle of twigs to search for a sign. There was Grandpa's plant-collecting bag – and there was Grandpa! He was streaked with mud and covered in cuts, with a big bruise on his forehead, but he was peacefully asleep, leaning against a rock. He must have somehow led the cow to safety and then sunk down, too tired to go another step.

Wilen knelt beside him, smiling, but when he took his grandfather's hand, he found that it was quite, quite cold.

Mother had to use Aunty Em's stove to cook the funeral feast. All the women helped out by bringing their biggest pots to replace the ones that Mother had lost in the mudslide. Uncle Rengu killed one of his surviving pigs and the men and boys cut short lengths of bamboo to cook Grandpa's favourite meal: pork and ginger baked inside bamboo sticks.

Toka and Tika caught a load of little fish to cook with rice. Everyone who wasn't cooking was helping to rebuild what the cyclone had destroyed.

Wilen escaped from all the bustle of preparations and went off into the forest on his own. The green and the quiet under the leaves comforted him. He knew that Grandpa was gone, but here in the company of the great trees he could still hear his voice.

"Without the forest, who would we be?"

"The forest gives us our soul."

Wilen knew that Grandpa was right. He didn't like Mr Patchap and the way he'd talked about killing elephants as if they were just pesky flies and cutting down the forest like a patch of unruly grass. But Denngu was right too. They had to live, they had to eat and now the cyclone had made that more difficult than ever. Wilen buried his face in his hands. It was all too difficult. Why couldn't things just stay the same?

A breeze crept in under the leaves and ruffled

Wilen's hair. He looked up and saw a little plant with toothed leaves and a yellow flower caught in a shaft of sunlight. It was a plant that Grandpa had often shown him. But now, for the very first time, Wilen remembered what it was for. He picked ten of its leaves and folded them carefully into his pocket. Then he ran back to the village and put the leaves into his mother's hands.

"Oh, Wilen!" she exclaimed. "How did you know? These are the healing leaves for Nono's cough!"

People came to the funeral feast from the villages all around and the talking and singing went on for hours. Father and Dax made a big bonfire and everyone sat in the firelight and smoke, remembering Grandpa and days gone past.

"He would have loved this," Mother said, with tears in her eyes.

A few days later, they scattered Grandpa's ashes on the only jhum field that the mudslide hadn't swept away. The rain spattered on the leaves and ran down their faces with the tears. The only person who didn't cry was Denngu. He stared at the ashes washing into the earth and looked as if he might just wash away too. Wilen stood beside him. He wanted to say something to make his uncle feel better, but he felt too bad himself to think of anything.

Mother looked at her youngest brother and shook her head. "I wish they hadn't quarrelled," she said sadly.

Father tucked Nono further inside his coat out of the rain. "Try not to worry," he said. "I have an idea that may help him."

Chapter Twelve

By tradition, Grandpa's *devadla* – the cloth that wrapped him when he was a newborn – must now be returned to Himandal, the village where he was born. It was far away on the other side of the province and with Nono to care for and so much work to be done in the village, neither Mother nor Rengu could be away. So Father's good idea was that Denngu and Wilen should make the journey. All the family agreed that this was a fine plan.

So, two days after they had sprinkled Grandpa's remains on the wet earth, Wilen and Denngu were getting off a bus, after twelve long hours of winding around hairpin bends, avoiding beeping lorries.

Wilen looked around. Grey clouds drifted like rags over the hills and a group of houses, built of brick and flattened tin cans, huddled from the wind. On the horizon, tall chimneys smudged the clouds darker with their smoke. There were no people to be seen anywhere, and no trees, just dead, yellow grass and the sad little houses crouching under the dull sky. A rusted sign saying "Himandal" showed that they were in the right place, in spite of its unpromising appearance. Wilen shivered. Was this really where Grandpa had grown up?

Denngu zipped up his biker jacket. "Well," he said, "let's get this done, shall we?"

They knocked on the door of the only house that showed any sign of life. A thread of smoke came from its chimney.

A high, wobbly voice called out, "Go away!"

Denngu knocked again.

"Go *away*!" the voice said, sounding even higher and more wobbly. "Didn't you hear the first time?"

"I'm sorry to disturb you, madam," Denngu called out, "but I am the youngest son of Jenak Achangitok Areng."

Wilen had never heard his grandfather's full name said out loud before. It sounded strange to him, but it worked like a charm on the owner of the wobbly voice.

The corrugated iron door scraped open and a tiny old lady stood before them, as fragile as a bird. She looked up intently into Denngu's face. "I can see you are Jenak's boy," she said. "But who's this?" And she poked Wilen in the chest with a trembling and very dirty finger.

"My sister's son," Denngu replied. "His grandson."

"Ah!" she said. "Well you'd better come in."

She gave the most enormous sigh and Wilen thought that he had never seen a person more tired.

The old lady hobbled down a dark corridor and into a small, cave-like room, lit with a single filthy light bulb and the flicker of a woodfire. On the floor stood a blackened pot of cooked rice with a spoon stuck in the middle.

Denngu and Wilen exchanged a look; it was clear that she hadn't eaten anything but rice in a long time.

The old lady sank down onto a chair and pointed to a low bench. "Sit there," she told them. "But put another log on the fire first. They're too heavy for me to lift more than one in a day."

Denngu did as she told him.

Wilen watched the log settle into the flames. It was a section cut from a huge, old tree. No one in Umiamara ever cut down trees that big just to burn. And no old lady in Umiamara would be on her own all day with nothing to eat but cold rice.

The old lady sighed again and looked into the fire. "I can guess why you're here," she said sadly. "He's dead, isn't he?"

Denngu answered, "Yes." It sounded as if the word scalded his throat.

"And you've come to bring his *devadla* to his mother's village?"

Denngu nodded. "We'd like to find..." he began.

But the old lady cut him off. "His relatives? All dead. Or just moved away. Long, long ago." She added, more kindly, "But I'll take the cloth for you. I knew him when we were young."

Silently, Denngu pulled out the *devadla* and put it into her hands. It seemed impossible that a person as large as Grandpa had been had once fitted inside this tiny piece of fabric.

The old lady took the *devadla* and rubbed it against her face. Then she folded it carefully and tucked it inside her jacket. "Come," she said. "There's something you should see."

The old lady told them to call her Ambi. She looked so small and alone as she led them across the bare, windy hillside down a stony track. It was slow progress, as walking clearly hurt her, but at last they reached a hollow and in it stood one enormous old tree. Ambi beckoned them close to it and leant her back against the trunk. She shut her eyes.

"Now," she said, "I have a story to tell you.

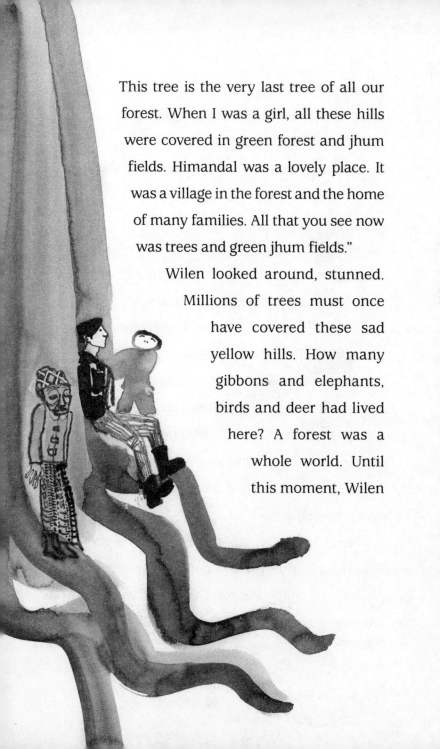

This tree is the very last tree of all our forest. When I was a girl, all these hills were covered in green forest and jhum fields. Himandal was a lovely place. It was a village in the forest and the home of many families. All that you see now was trees and green jhum fields."

Wilen looked around, stunned. Millions of trees must once have covered these sad yellow hills. How many gibbons and elephants, birds and deer had lived here? A forest was a whole world. Until this moment, Wilen hadn't understood how a whole world could disappear so entirely. Would Umiamara look like this one day? He shivered to think of it.

Denngu stood between the tree's great roots, his face pinched and pale, and stared at the bare hills as if it hurt him to look.

Ambi went on. "The forest gave us wood to build, medicines to heal and animals to eat. It brought rain to fill our rivers and to water our crops. But little by little, we cut it down to grow more crops, to mine for coal, to make money."

Ambi touched Denngu's arm and looked into his stricken face. "Your father, Jenak," she told him, "he warned us. *The coal will run out,* he said. *The soil will lose its goodness and no rain will come.* He warned us and warned us. But he was only young and no one listened.

"And one day, all the forest *was* gone. The coal *did* run out, the soil *did* die, the rains *did* fail. Just as he said. People had to leave or starve. And now there is nothing. Nothing and nobody.

Just me and the old tree, waiting to die."

She opened her eyes and stood away from the tree. "That's all I have to say. Now go home."

The bus drove on through the night. Wilen was exhausted. He could have slept standing up in the aisle. From time to time, he woke and found Denngu staring wide-eyed at the black window. He loved his uncle still, but now Wilen knew that he must try to win the fight that Grandpa had lost so long ago.

As they got off the bus the next morning in Tura, Wilen pulled out the paper money that had been burning in his pocket ever since Denngu had given it to him, and thrust it back into his uncle's hands.

Chapter Thirteen

When Wilen got back to Umiamara, there were just four more days until the big meeting with Mr Patchap – four days for Wilen to find a way to defeat him and stop Umiamara turning into a desert of dead grass like Himandal.

Children and young people were staying home to help with the cyclone repairs, so there was lots of time to listen to the village talk – lots of time to hear that the whole village was leaning like a tree being felled, ready to fall into Mr Patchap's lap and sign away their forest for ever.

The more he heard people talk about the houses they would build and the motorbikes they would buy with the money that Mr Patchap's deal would surely bring, the worse Wilen felt. It seemed unstoppable, as irresistible as the cyclone itself. So when Father offered to take him into Tura, on a visit to the town council offices to report on the cyclone, Wilen was glad to escape.

He sat in the waiting area outside the room where Father was having his meeting. His legs stuck to the plastic chair and a fly buzzed loudly against the window. Feeling half asleep, he began to flick through the pages of the council's newsletter that was lying on the desk. He was hardly paying attention, so he very nearly didn't notice the photo at the bottom of the inside page. But once he had seen it, he was wide awake.

It showed a tall man in a green uniform shaking hands with a village Nokma. Around them, a crowd of smiling school children held tiny seedling trees in pots.

Nokengaber village benefits from a new tree-planting scheme. Villagers will be paid to plant and care for trees.

Wilen's heart turned like a leaf. What if Umiamara could be paid to plant and care for trees instead of cutting them down?

His eyes raked the page to find out more, but

there was nothing. A lady sat behind a desk in the corner of the room. Blushing and trembling with embarrassment, Wilen carried the newspaper to her. He pointed to the man in the photograph and managed to growl out one useful word, "Who?"

The lady might have ignored the gangling, almost wordless boy in front of her. But she didn't. She was kind; she smiled and said, "Oh, that's Mr Chatterjee. His office is on the top floor."

Wilen's long legs wobbled. This was his opportunity to get a business associate of his own, one who might offer a real alternative to Mr Patchap's poisonous deal. Without giving himself the chance to wonder what he would say when he got there, or how he would manage to say it, Wilen leapt up all six flights of stairs to Mr Chatterjee's floor.

Mr Chatterjee might not have been in his office; he seldom was. But on this particular Tuesday afternoon when Wilen knocked, as if by a miracle, a voice called, "Come in!"

* * *

The evening of the big meeting came. Wilen felt sick. While Mother and Aunty Em cooked a load of tapioca root, he cuddled Nono because her little warm body on his chest made him feel a bit calmer. He thought about telling Mother and Father what he had planned, but he knew that a surprise could be powerful. Denngu had taught him that.

At last, night came. Pools of lantern light wound up the paths across the hillside to the Nokma's house. People spoke quietly and politely nibbled at the tapioca root. Everyone was very solemn.

Denngu was going to come with Mr Patchap. People watched out anxiously for the appearance of the big black car. But there was no sign of it. Wilen watched out too, but he was looking for another vehicle altogether.

At last, headlights showed in the darkness. Wilen's heart leapt, but when Mr Patchap's monster 4x4 drew into the yard, it dropped to the bottom of his chest. How could he fight the battle alone?

Mr Patchap got out and explained that Denngu

would be unable to come to the meeting. Mother and Father exchanged looks, but really no one was surprised. Denngu had set up the deal and now he must have moved on to other things, just like he always did.

The villagers greeted Mr Patchap eagerly and watched with hungry eyes as he drew official-looking papers from his pocket and laid them on the table, ready for the villagers to sign. The decision had been made. It seemed that no one wanted to talk about it any more. After all that they'd lost to the rain, the elephants and the cyclone, what choice did they have?

Wilen gazed desperately down the track, but there wasn't a glimmer of headlights anywhere. It was now or never. He *had* to find his voice. "I'd like…" his voice squeaked. He tried again. "…to say something," his voice growled.

Mr Patchap looked up. "Did I hear one of your famous gibbons making a noise then?" The man laughed at his own joke, but Wilen noticed that no one else did. That gave him courage. He stood up on a chair so that his small voice could carry just a little further. "No," growled Wilen. "It was me."

He saw Father looking at him in astonishment and Mother at the back smiling as if she knew some lovely secret. She had picked Relip up so that he could see his big brother. Relip, for once, had stopped talking.

Mr Patchap stood up. "I don't think we need to listen to the opinions of children."

Mother looked sternly at Mr Patchap. "In our culture," she said, "everyone's opinion is heard. Carry on, son."

Wilen took a deep breath and stopped worrying that his voice swooped in pitch on every other word. It didn't matter what people thought about him any more. What mattered was what he had to say. He shut his eyes tight to squeeze out the nervousness and spoke up.

"I went to Himandal, Grandpa's village," he said, as loudly as he could, "and everyone had left except one old lady, who lived alone with no one to make her fire or cook her dinner. She was the loneliest person I've ever seen."

It had gone very, very quiet.

Wilen went on, "She showed us a tree. One tree. *Just one tree.* It was the last tree left out of all the forest that once covered those hills, like our forest covers our hills. In her village – my grandfather's village – they cut their trees to grow crops and mine coal. And even though he was young then, my grandpa warned them what would happen. He told them that the soil would get tired and the coal would run out and then the money would run out and everyone would have to leave the land.

"And he was right. No one lives in that village now. No one except one lonely, lonely old woman."

Wilen took a big breath and opened his eyes. He didn't feel scared any more. He just wanted everyone to listen. He looked round at all the faces, at all the eyes fixed on him, and he told them, "If we cut down our forest like Mr Patchap wants, we will lose

our elephants, our gibbons, our homes, our food, our rain. And worst of all, we'll lose each other!"

Denngu had always known how to make a good entrance. He stepped into the silence that Wilen's words had created, clapping.

"Well done, Wilen. That was wonderful, Nephew."

Wilen's heart fell. Handsome, clever Uncle Denngu was about to make a fool of him. But then Wilen saw that his uncle wasn't laughing. In fact, tears stood in his eyes.

"Since I spoke to you all about the deal with Mr Patchap here," Denngu said, "I've had a change of heart. I've seen that my father was right. I've also found out that Mr Patchap isn't a very nice man to be in business with."

Denngu turned his face to the light to show that his cheek was cut and bruised.

"This is what Mr Patchap does to people who disagree with him."

The villagers gasped in horror.

Mr Patchap squirmed in his chair.

"So I am happy to tell you that my clever nephew has found a much better partner for Umia-mara," said Denngu. "I think you should hear what Mr Chatterjee has to say."

Mr Chatterjee appeared around the end of the shelter. "Apologies for my lateness," he said. "My Land

Rover is stuck a mile down your track! Denngu was kind enough to give me a lift on his motorbike."

Mr Chatterjee's accent was unfamiliar and hard to understand at first. "He's from Delhi," Denngu whispered into his sister's ear. "He can't help it."

But the villagers were very pleased when they heard what Mr Chatterjee had to say.

"Your forest here holds so many animals and plants that it is like a storehouse of treasures. These are valued across India and all the world. My organization wishes to help you to be guardians of that treasure."

Mr Chatterjee's organization would pay the people of Umiamara to plant trees on old jhum plots and on the mudslide where all the trees had been swept away; it would give them bee hives and a chicken house so that they didn't have to cut down more and more forest to earn a living.

Everyone was so busy smiling and shaking Mr Chatterjee's hand and congratulating Wilen that no one noticed Mr Patchap, his driver and his big, black car slinking away.

"There is one more thing," said Mr Chatterjee, shouting to make himself heard above the excited villagers. "It concerns elephants."

Immediately everyone fell silent.

"I know you have had many problems with elephants." Mr Chatterjee shook his head sadly and then went on, "Umiamara is close to the place where they cross the river, as you know. But if we restore the forest on both sides of that crossing, elephants can travel without the need to stray into crops and villages and cause a nuisance. We wish to create what we call a green corridor along which they may travel between the two forest reserves," Mr Chatterjee explained earnestly. "You could call it," he added, with a small smile at his own wit, "an Elephant Road."

Grandpa's voice echoed in Wilen's heart.

We live on the elephant road between elephant palaces.

Epilogue

Wilen helped Silmi onto the ladder. He still thought of her as Nono, but at seven she got *very* cross with *anyone* who called her that!

"Don't be afraid," he told her. "I'm right behind you."

"I'm not afraid," she said, tossing her plaits at him. "I climb up to the lookout all the time!"

They reached the lookout and sat at the far end gazing out over the hills and valleys.

"Tell me about the landslide again, Wilen!" Silmi loved to hear the stories about the village's most dramatic year.

"It was right there, from Mother's house down the valley and over the stream."

"You can hardly tell now."

"We planted trees on it when you were one, so they are almost as tall as this lookout now."

It was true. The ugly scar was healed and covered with vigorous young forest, full of life.

"Will the trees we planted today grow that fast?"

Wilen laughed. "By the time you go to high school, it'll be a proper forest. And by the time you get married…"

Silmi giggled and punched her brother in the arm.

"…there will be gibbons singing in its tree tops."

They sat for a moment watching the pink sky and listening to the evening calls of birds.

"You're going tomorrow, aren't you?"

"You know I am, Silmi. I have to go to live in my wife's village. It's the tradition. And it's nearer college for my forestry course."

"You're sad to leave, aren't you?"

Wilen nodded.

"I'll take care of the forest, you know," said Silmi. "You don't need to worry. I'll be Nokma after Mummy and I'll plant so many trees. You just wait!" She squeezed his hand. "Look!" she breathed. "There!"

Amongst the young trees on the mudslide, five

elephants were moving. Slowly and calmly, with no need to worry or rush, they were walking up the road to their palace.

A herd of Asian elephants
getting ready to cross a river

LIVING WITH ELEPHANTS

There are two kinds of elephants in the world: African and Asian. The elephants in this book are Asian elephants and although they are the slightly smaller of the two kinds, they are still very, very large animals. Females weigh as much as a 4x4 car and males almost twice that. A body that size needs a lot to eat and drink — around 100kg of leaves, roots, bark and fruits, and about 100 litres of water — every day. Elephants walk 8km or more each day to find all they need, and they travel much longer distances to find food and water at different times of year. They have big brains and long memories to help them remember where to find the best fruiting trees or sources of water. Sometimes, the routes that they travel between places that provide food in different seasons have been used for generations, and are so well worn that they are called elephant roads.

Which all adds up to the fact that elephants don't fit into small spaces. They need lots of unspoilt natural habitat to survive. Unfortunately, all over their range, from China through India to Sri Lanka, that is just what is disappearing under cities and roads, farmland and factories. So there are only 50,000 Asian elephants left in the wild and the number is falling all the time.

One of the big problems is that, even where there is good elephant habitat, forest or grassland, with plenty of food and water, it is often split up into islands with villages, towns and farmland in between. Or humans may set up houses, roads or farms on what was once an elephant road. Either way, elephants must travel through the human habitat to get to their habitat, which almost always spells trouble. Human crops are like super yummy versions of an elephant's wild food, so it isn't surprising that elephants will eat them when they can, bringing them into conflict with humans. Every year, around 300 people in India are killed by elephants. A similar number of elephants are killed by people, because people just get fed up with the crops being stolen and their relatives being trodden on, even by accident.

The solution is to link up the bits of natural elephant habitat with undisturbed natural habitat – green corridors – and keep people out of established elephant roads. Elephants can then move about without having to pass through farmland, villages or towns and be tempted to raid crops or generally cause a nuisance. This is not as easy as it sounds in a country like India, where there are over a billion people who all need a place to live and food to eat. But in some parts of India, these solutions are being made to work by local people helped by conservation organizations such as Wildlife Trust of India (WTI) and the UK-based World Land Trust (WLT).

The Garo Hills, an area in the far north-east of India, are stunningly beautiful – rolling hills covered in rainforest, and with a healthy population of wild elephants. The Garo people who live there practise slash and burn cultivation, known as jhumming. They clear a small area of forest, grow crops for a few years, then let it return to forest. This system worked well for many generations. The jhum plots provided crops, and the

A rice field and
storage hut on stilts in the Garo Hills

forest provided wood for fuel and building, plants for
flavours and medicines, meat and fish for food. But as
the human population rose, more and more forest was
'jhummed' and old jhum plots were being cleared again
before they'd had time to regrow. The Garo people had
to cut down more and more of the forest that was so
important to them, just to survive, or turn to mining

to make money. As the forest shrank, so elephants and humans came into conflict with each other, with fatal results on both sides.

Now WTI supported by WLT are helping Garo villagers to find other ways to make a living that take the pressure off the forest, such as rearing chickens or pigs, or keeping bees. Villagers can also earn money from planting trees and caring for them, so that they regrow

A lookout hut for
spotting elephants in crops

forest, joining up the patchwork of existing woodland and creating green corridors that elephants, gibbons and other wildlife can use in safety. More and more villages are joining in and proudly planting new forest and protecting the huge ancient trees of the old.

The aim of all this is to create a whole series of green corridors that connect the elephants' route between

Children from a village in the Garo Hills

two big forest reserves in the National Parks and allow them to cross rivers and move around the forested hills in peace.

The Garo people love their forest and are very proud of their ability to protect it for the benefit of everyone in their part of India. Their young people want to safeguard the forest because they see it as an essential part of who they are. But there are still many threats to the future of the forests of the Garo Hills and to elephant habitats across India. What we can do is support organizations that help the Garo people, and others like them, to hold on to their precious forest and the human communities that depend on it.

"I'm coming to get you," Pedru told the lion.

THE LION WHO STOLE MY ARM
Mozambique, Africa

Pedru hopes he's strong enough to kill the lion
who took his arm. But will he have the strength to
turn his back on revenge?

WALKING THE BEAR
Bhopal, Central India

When Zaki is given twin bear cubs to train as
dancing bears he decides to return them to
the wild instead. But teaching bears to be bears
is harder than he expected.

Manuela hugged the baby manatee.
"Don't die!" she told it.

MANATEE BABY

NICOLA DAVIES

MANATEE BABY
Amazon Basin, Colombia

When her father kills a manatee, Manuela
promises to return its orphaned baby to the river
one day. But she finds that promises are
hard to keep.